Miss Henn

and

Family

Miss Henn and Family is written by Orane Lewis
Copyright 2006, Orane Lewis

Published and Printed by:
Lifevest Publishing
4901 E. Dry Creek Rd., #170
Centennial, CO 80122
www.lifevestpublishing.com

Printed in China

I.S.B.N. 1-59879-141-9

Miss Henn and Family

by Orane Lewis

Illustrations
by Dianne Vest and Amanda

Miss Henn, Mr. Roos and their four little chicks live on a farm. The farm also has a horse, pigs, goats, cows, a dog and a fishing pond.

Miss Henn and her family are famous on the farm, and they get a lot of attention.

Every morning between 6:00 and 6:30 AM Miss Henn and her little chicks get up to roam all over the farm. Mr. Roos is never far away, keeping a close watch on the family. Miss Henn leads the way to the barn with her little chicks right behind her. Next to the barn is the feeding area for the family, the place where they find their food and water. Their meals consist mainly of crushed corn along with other nutritious food to keep them healthy. It is also in the barn that Miss Henn lays her eggs and hatches her chicks.

After eating, Miss Henn and her family walk around the farm, stopping from time to time to pick on leaves. The water grass is a big favorite for the family, the leaves there are very tasty. Miss Henn is always teaching her young chicks how to search for worms and ants hiding in the ground. She uses her feet to scratch in the ground and her well-designed beak pulls the food out of the ground.

Mr. Roos is not as active in teaching the chicks how to search for food or to be on alert for predators, but he is always close by to keep watch over his family.

Whenever Mr. Roos is not around keeping a watchful eye on the family, you will find him at the far end of the farm by a dead tree that's laying on the ground. He picks in it to search for his favorite ants, the red ants. When he finds them he makes a sound to alert the family and they come quickly to get their share of the red ants.

After roaming the entire farm for most of the day, it is now time for the family to head back to their sleeping area. Even though they have a coop, they rarely stay in there, choosing instead to spend the night in a storage pen next to the pigs. At night Miss Henn keeps her chicks warm by covering them with her wings.

Miss Henn and her family have a close relationship with the pigs on the farm. Sometimes they even eat some of the left over feed in the pig pen. The young chicks jump on the backs of the pigs and enjoy a little ride as they move about in the pen.

From time to time Miss Henn and her family have to run for cover while walking around the farm. Chicken hawks can dive down very fast when flying over the farm and can snatch up their prey with their strong feet.

No one is really sure where this hawk comes from or if there is more than one. Only one thing is for sure; the hawk must not be staying close by since it only comes around a few times each year.

Whenever there is a bird flying in the sky, Mr. Roos and Miss Henn sound the alarm and the whole family runs quickly for cover. They fear the bird in the sky may be the chicken hawk hunting for its next meal.

Even though most of the farm is open space, and there aren't a lot of trees, Miss Henn, Mr. Roos and the chicks still move about freely. They roam all over the property as if they know very well that they are the center of attention on the farm.

Once a month Jaland and Jada visit the farm to see their God-parents, Wayne and Cindy. They also love to see Miss Henn and her family. Jada loves to play with the chicks and feed them. She has also nick-named one of the chicks "friend" because that special little chick always follows her around. Could it be that this little chick is only following Jada around because of the feed she gives it?

Jaland is more into playing with the dog. His name is Speedy, and he seems to enjoy spending time playing with Jaland too. Speedy earned his name because of his speed and the wonderful job he does chasing off any unwelcome visitors. Just like Mr. Roos, he spends a lot of time watching over the animals on the farm.

Around 4:30 AM every morning, Mr. Roos lets it be known what a big guy he is on the farm by crowing "cock-a-doodle-doo" very loudly. All the animals on the farm used to be annoyed by this loud noise, but over time they have all become used to Mr. Roos's cock-a-doodle-doo sound.

It is now four weeks since the chicks were born, and everyone is talking about how much they have grown. Soon they will be on their own.

Miss Henn has prepared them very well for the day when they will no longer be following her around all day. They will still remain a family, but the chicks will roam the farm without Mr. Roos or Miss Henn at their side.

Now that the chicks have grown up, you can tell that there are two little Miss Henns. Their names are Evernes and Gee Gee.

There are also two little Mr. Roos. Their names are Gus and Giggy.

In about a year there will be several new additions to this family when Evernes and Gee Gee start having chicks of their own.

Now the four chicks are all grown up and no longer need the attention of their parents. Each morning they go off in different directions.

The little chick named friend by Jada (Evernes) still makes her way to the feeding area next to the barn every morning. The others still go to the pig pen and the feeding area for the goats.

It now appears that soon Miss Henn will again be adding chicks to the family. She has been seen making several visits behind the stock of hay.

Yes indeed, Miss Henn is laying her eggs and once again there could be several little chicks added to the family.

Jaland and Jada are making another visit to the farm, and as usual Jaland plays with Speedy the dog and Jada tries to find the little chick she named Friend (Evernes).

With the help of her Godmother Cindy, Jada manages to track down her Friend, who was picking on the leaves of her favorite grass. Jada is happy to see the chick once again.

Since the little chicks are now all grown they no longer spend the night with Miss Henn and Mr. Roos. Evernes and Gee Gee have made the coop their sleeping area, while Gus and Giggy spend the night in a tree not far from the barn.

It is a mid-summer night and the sky opens up for the rain to come pouring down. Then comes the flashes of lightning and the rumbling of thunder.

Surely the chicks are scared as they have never had such an experience before.

The following morning there was no crowing cock-a-doodle-doo from Mr. Roos at 4:30 AM. Surely he did not sleep well during the heavy rain and the loud thunder.

Thank goodness! The next morning everything is calm, and for the first time in several weeks Miss Henn, Mr. Roos and the family are all seen together at their feeding area next to the barn.

To Order Copies of

Miss Henn and Family

by **Orane Lewis**

I.S.B.N. 1-59879-141-9

Order Online at:
www.authorstobelievein.com

By Phone Toll Free at:
1-877-843-1007